# Enid Blyton's
# NODDY
# Has an Afternoon Off

## BBC CHILDREN'S BOOKS

It was a peaceful day in Toyland. Noddy had been busy all morning and now he was enjoying a rest in his garden. Suddenly, a ball landed in his lap.

Master Tubby Bear looked over the garden wall.

"Master Tubby, this is my afternoon off! Do be more careful," said Noddy as he tossed the ball back over the wall.

"Thank you," said Master Tubby.

Noddy sat down again and closed his eyes. But before he could get to sleep, naughty Tubby Bear threw the ball again and it landed on Noddy's head.

"I've had enough of this," said Noddy. "Keep your ball in your own garden!" he shouted, and he threw the ball back over the wall.

"Look what you've done!" said Master Tubby. "You've knocked my father's prize red apple off his tree. He'll be furious."

"Oh, no! What shall I do?" Noddy asked.

"Well, you could get another apple and stick it on to the tree," suggested Tubby.

"Big-Ears will be able to help," said Noddy. "He's got lots of apples."

So Noddy set off to see Big-Ears.

Noddy told Big-Ears what had happened.

"I shall search through my apple store until I find a great big, ripe, red, juicy apple for you," said Big-Ears. "I wonder if you could do me a favour while you're waiting, and ask Mr Sparks if I can borrow his ladder?"

"Of course I will," agreed Noddy. "I'll go right away."

Noddy found Mr Sparks and asked him if he could borrow the ladder.

"You may take the ladder when I've mended this guttering," said Mr Sparks. "While you're waiting, perhaps you could do me a favour. Will you go to the farm and fetch me six eggs?"

"I will go right away," said Noddy before he drove off.

Mr and Mrs Straw explained that they only had five eggs so far.

"But Mr Sparks wants *six* eggs," said Noddy.

"We'll have to wait for another one," said Mrs Straw. "Would you fetch my new rope from Sammy Sailor while you're waiting?"

So Noddy set off.

When Noddy got to the quayside, he asked Sammy
Sailor for the rope.

"I'll have to look for it in my store," Sammy said. "While
you're waiting you can drive to Dinah Doll's stall and
fetch a set of new plates for the ship's cook."

And Noddy drove away.

When Noddy got to Dinah Doll's stall, he was very
pleased to find that she had the plates ready for him.
"These are the plates Sammy wants," Dinah said as she
piled them up into Noddy's arms.

"There are ever such a lot of them," grumbled Noddy. "I suppose I'd better take them right away," he said, but the plates started to rattle and wobble as he walked off. "Do be careful!" called Dinah. "Please don't break any."

"Look out, Noddy," cautioned Mr Plod. "Those plates look very dangerous to me. They are wobbling all over the place."

"Look out," said the Clockwork Mouse. "You're going to drop all those plates, and then the ship's cook will be cross!"

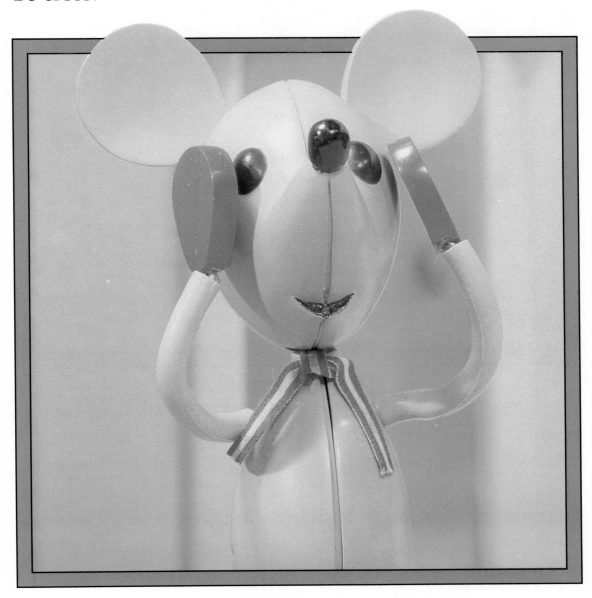

It was no good. Noddy rattled and wobbled his way back to Dinah Doll's stall.

"I must pack these plates properly," Dinah decided. "You can do me a favour while you wait. Will you go and fetch the silver teapot Miss Pink Cat has promised to lend me, please?"

"Of course," said Noddy.

"I could not let you carry my valuable silver teapot," said Pink Cat. "You would put grimy finger prints on it."

"If you let me take it I'll do you a favour," pleaded Noddy.

"Very well. You may go to the station and fetch a parcel I'm expecting. It contains a set of the finest dusters."

Noddy collected the parcel. "Big-Ears – ladder, Mr Sparks – eggs, Mr and Mrs Straw – rope . . ." said Noddy as he went back to his car.

"What are you talking about?" interrupted Martha Monkey.

"It's a list I have to remember of all the favours I'm doing for people," explained Noddy.

"You can do me a favour," Martha said. "You can give me a lift into town."

As he drove, Noddy kept repeating his list. "Mr Sparks – eggs, Mr and Mrs Straw – rope!"

"Big-Ears – dusters, Miss Pink Cat – plates," said Martha Monkey.

"Be quiet, Martha!" said Noddy. "You're confusing me. Miss Pink Cat – plates. Mr Sparks – lift into town. Oh no, that's not right."

"Mr and Mrs Straw – ladder. Mr Sparks – plates!" called Martha.

"Stop it!" said Noddy. "I've got to take these dusters to Sammy Sailor."

Noddy pulled up at the quayside.

"I've got your rope, Noddy!" said Sammy, passing him the new rope.

"Thank you, Sammy. I've got your dusters," Noddy replied.

"I don't want dusters," said Sammy.

But Noddy wasn't listening. "I wish I could remember where to go next," he sighed. "Big-Ears – eggs? No, that's not right. Mr Straw – dusters?"

"Dinah Doll – ladder.
Miss Pink Cat – rope,"
butted in Martha Monkey.
   "That's it! Miss Pink
Cat," said Noddy, and
he quickly drove off.
   "Don't forget my plates!"
called Sammy Sailor.

But when Noddy got to Miss Pink Cat's house, she wasn't very pleased. "How can I clean my best china with a rope? I want dusters," she said, crossly.

"Then who wants this rope?" asked Noddy. "Big-Ears, that's it," he said, and rushed off.

"Don't forget my dusters!" called Miss Pink Cat.

"Big-Ears, I've brought your rope," Noddy called when he got to Big-Ears' house.

"I don't need a rope, Noddy. I need a ladder," said Big-Ears, rather puzzled.

"Oh, Big-Ears. I'm doing so many favours for so many people. Martha Monkey made me so confused I can't remember who asked for what," said Noddy.

"Calm down, Noddy. Now, who gave you the rope?" asked Big-Ears.

"It was Sammy Sailor," replied Noddy.

"Then you must go and see Sammy," advised Big-Ears. "Then you can retrace your steps."

"Thank you, Big-Ears. I'll go right away," said Noddy.

It was so late that it had started to getting dark by the time Noddy left Big-Ears' house. Poor Noddy drove all over Toyland. He took the rope to Mr and Mrs Straw, the teapot to Dinah Doll, the plates to Sammy Sailor, the dusters to Miss Pink Cat, the eggs to Mr Sparks . . .

. . . and finally he borrowed the
ladder and took it to Big-Ears.

"Thank you for fetching the
ladder, Noddy," said Big-Ears.
"Here's your great big, ripe, red,
juicy apple. I've put it in a little
bag for you."

Noddy yawned. "I wonder why I wanted a great big, ripe, red juicy apple?"

"For Mr Tubby Bear," laughed Big-Ears.

"Of course! I will take it right away," said Noddy, and he left.

When Noddy got back to Mr Tubby Bear's garden, he tried to reach up quietly to put the apple on the tree. Suddenly, a light went on.

"Noddy! What are you doing?" said Mr Tubby.

"You're going to be very cross," said Noddy, hanging his head. "I was throwing Master Tubby's ball back from my garden and I accidentally knocked your prize apple off your tree. I was trying to stick this apple in its place so you wouldn't notice. I'm very sorry."

"But I don't have a prize apple. At this time of year, these small apples are only just starting to grow," said Mr Tubby Bear. "I think Master Tubby was playing a trick on you."

"I've spent my afternoon off racing round Toyland for nothing," said Noddy, crossly.

"I'm so tired and hungry," he added.

"You do have a great big, ripe, red, juicy apple," said Mr Tubby Bear. "I'm sorry Master Tubby played such a silly trick."

"Never mind," said Noddy, biting into his apple. "I've worked so hard today, I think I'll have another afternoon off tomorrow!"

Published by BBC Children's Books
a division of BBC Worldwide Publishing
Woodlands, 80 Wood Lane, London W12 0TT

First published 1996
Reprinted 1996

ISBN 0 563 40531 7

Typeset in 17/21 pt Garamond by BBC Children's Books
Printed and bound in Great Britain by Cambus Litho, East Kilbride
Colour separations by DOT Gradations, Chelmsford